THE HANDS OF
MR. OTTERMOLE

BY

THOMAS BURKE

British Library Cataloguing-in-Publication Data
A catalogue record for this book is available from the
British Library

CONTENTS

THOMAS BURKE

Thomas Burke was born in Clapham, London in 1886. His father died when he was very young, and at the age of ten he was removed to a home for middle-class boys who were "respectably descended but without adequate means to their support." Burke published his first piece of writing—a short story entitled 'The Bellamy Diamonds'—in 1901, when he was just fifteen. However, proper recognition came in 1916, with the publication of *Limehouse Nights*, a collection of melodramatic short stories set amongst the immigrant population of London's Chinatown. *Limehouse Nights* was serialized in three British periodicals, *The English Review, Colour* and *The New Witness*, and received positive attention from reviewers and a number of authors, including H. G. Wells. It also sparked something of a controversy, however, and was initially banned by libraries due to the scandalous interracial relationships it portrayed between Chinese men and white women.

It was these portrayals of London's Chinatown that Burke is best-remembered for. However, there is some degree of confusion over how much of Burke's writing was based in fact; as literary critic Anne Witchard states, most of what we know about Burke's life is based on works that "purport to be autobiographical, yet contain far more invention than truth." Whatever the truth, there is no doubt that, in his day, Burke was regarded as the foremost chronicler of London's Chinatown at the turn-of-the-century. Burke told newspaper journalists that he had "sat at the feet of Chinese philosophers who kept opium dens to learn from the lips that could frame only broken English, the secrets, good and evil, of the mysterious East," and these journalists almost uniformly took him at his word.

Burke continued to use descriptions of urban London life as a focus of his writing throughout his life. Off the back of *Limehouse Nights*, Burke published the thematically similar *Twinkletoes* in 1918, and *More Limehouse Nights* in 1921. However, he was a prolific author who tried his hand at a number of different genres. He semi-regularly published essays on the London environment, including pieces such as 'The Real East End' and 'London in My Times', and during the thirties even tried his hand at horror fiction. Indeed, in 1949, shortly after his death, Burke's short story 'The Hands of Ottermole' was voted the best mystery of all time by critics. Burke also influenced the burgeoning film industry in Hollywood; D W Griffith, for example, used the short story 'The Chink and the Child' from *Limehouse Nights* (1917) as basis for his silent movie, *Broken Blossoms* (1919), and Charlie Chaplin derived 'A Dog's Life' (1918) from the same book.

THE HANDS OF MR OTTERMOLE

At six o'clock of a January evening Mr Whybrow was walking home through the cobweb alleys of London's East End. He had left the golden clamour of the great High Street to which the tram had brought him from the river and his daily work, and was now in the chess-board of byways that is called Mallon End. None of the rush and gleam of the High Street trickled into these byways. A few paces south—a flood-tide of life, foaming and beating. Here—only slow shuffling figures and muffled pulses. He was in the sink of London, the last refuge of European vagrants.

As though in tune with the street's spirit, he too walked slowly, with head down. It seemed that he was pondering some pressing trouble, but he was not. He had no trouble. He was walking slowly because he had been on his feet all day, and he was bent in abstraction because he was wondering whether the Missis would have herrings for his tea, or haddock; and he was trying to decide which would be the more tasty on a night like this. A wretched night it was, of damp and mist, and the mist wandered into his throat and his eyes, and the damp had settled on pavement and roadway, and where the sparse lamplight fell it sent up a greasy sparkle that chilled one to look at. By contrast it made his speculations more agreeable, and made him ready for that tea—whether herring or haddock. His eye turned from the glum bricks that made his horizon, and went forward half a mile. He saw a gas-lit kitchen, a flamy fire and a spread tea-table. There was toast in the hearth and a singing kettle on the side and a piquant effusion of herrings, or maybe of haddock, or perhaps sausages. The vision gave his aching feet a throb of energy. He shook imperceptible damp from his shoulders, and hastened towards its reality.

But Mr Whybrow wasn't going to get any tea that evening—or any other evening. Mr Whybrow was going to die. Somewhere within a hundred yards of him another man was walking: a man much like Mr Whybrow and much like any other man, but without the only quality that enables mankind to live peaceably together and not as madmen in a jungle. A man with a dead heart eating into itself and bringing forth the foul organisms that arise from death and corruption. And that thing in man's shape, on a whim or a settled idea—one cannot know—had said within himself that Mr Whybrow should never taste another herring. Not that Mr Whybrow had injured him. Not that he had any dislike of Mr Whybrow. Indeed, he knew nothing of him save as a familiar figure about the streets. But, moved by a force that had taken possession of his empty cells, he had picked on Mr Whybrow with that blind choice that makes us pick one restaurant table that has nothing to mark it from four of five other tables, or one apple from a dish of half a dozen equal apples; or that drives Nature to send a cyclone upon one corner of this planet, and destroy five hundred lives in that corner, and leave another five hundred in the same corner unharmed. So this man had picked on Mr Whybrow, as he might have picked on you or me, had we been within his daily observation; and even now he was creeping through the blue-toned streets, nursing his large white hands, moving ever closer to Mr Whybrow's tea-table, and so closer to Mr Whybrow himself.

He wasn't, this man, a bad man. Indeed, he had many of the social and amiable qualities, and passed as a respectable man, as most successful criminals do. But the thought had come into his mouldering mind that he would like to murder somebody, and, as he held no fear of God or man, he was going to do it, and would then go home to *his* tea. I don't say that flippantly, but as a statement of fact. Strange as it may seem to the humane, murderers must and do sit down to meals after a murder. There is no reason why they shouldn't, and many reasons why they should. For one thing, they need to keep their physical and mental vitality at full beat for the business of covering their crime. For another, the strain of their effort makes them hungry, and satisfaction at the accomplishment of a desired thing brings a feeling of relaxation towards human pleasures. It is accepted among non-murderers that the murderer is always overcome by fear for his safety and horror at his act; but this type is rare. His own safety is, of course, his immediate concern, but vanity is a marked quality of most murderers, and that, together with the thrill of conquest, makes him confident that he can secure it, and when he has restored his strength with food he goes about securing it as a young hostess goes about the arranging of her first big dinner—a little anxious, but no more. Criminologists and detectives tell us that *every* murderer, however intelligent or cunning, always makes one slip in his tactics—one little slip that brings the affair home to him. But that is only half-true. It is true only of the murderers who are caught. Scores of murderers are not caught: therefore scores of murderers do not make any mistake at all. This man didn't.

As for horror or remorse, prison chaplains, doctors and lawyers have told us that of murderers they have interviewed under condemnation and the shadow of death, only one here and there has expressed any contrition for his act, or shown any sign of mental misery. Most of them display only exasperation at having been caught when so many have gone undiscovered, or indignation at being condemned for a perfectly reasonable act. However normal and humane they may have been before the murder, they are utterly without conscience after it. For what is conscience? Simply a polite nickname for superstition, which is a polite nickname for fear. Those who associate remorse with murder are, no doubt, basing their ideas on the world-legend of the remorse of Cain, or are projecting their own frail minds into the mind of the murderer, and getting false reactions. Peaceable folk cannot hope to make contact with this mind, for they are not merely different in mental type from the murderer; they are different in their personal chemistry and construction. Some men can and do kill, not one man, but two or three, and go calmly about their daily affairs. Other men could not, under the most agonizing provocation, bring themselves even to wound. It is men of this sort who imagine the murderer in torments of remorse and fear of the law, whereas he is actually sitting down to his tea.

The man with the large white hands was as ready for his tea as Mr Whybrow was, but he had something to do before he went to it. When he had done that something, and made no mistake about it, he would be even more ready for it, and would go to it as comfortably as he went to it the day before, when his hands were stainless.

Walk on, then, Mr Whybrow, walk on; and as you walk, look your last upon the familiar features of your nightly journey. Follow your jack-o'-lantern tea-table. Look well upon its warmth and colour and kindness; feed your eyes with it, and tease your nose with its gentle domestic odours; for you will never sit down to it. Within ten minutes' pacing of you a pursuing phantom has spoken in his heart, and you are doomed. There you go—you and phantom—two nebulous dabs of mortality, moving through green air along pavements of powder-blue, the one to kill, the other to be killed. Walk on. Don't annoy your burning feet by hurrying, for the more slowly you walk, the longer you will breathe the green air of this January dusk, and see the dreamy lamplight and the little shops, and hear the agreeable commerce of the London crowd and the haunting pathos of the street-organ. These things are dear to you, Mr Whybrow. You don't know it now, but in fifteen minutes you will have two seconds in which to realize how inexpressibly dear they are.

Walk on, then, across this crazy chess-board. You are in Lagos Street now, among the tents of the wanderers of Eastern Europe. A minute or so, and you are in Loyal Lane, among the lodging-houses that shelter the useless and the beaten of London's camp-followers. The lane holds the smell of them, and its soft darkness seems heavy with the wail of the futile. But you are not sensitive to impalpable things, and you plod through it, unseeing, as you do every evening, and come to Blean Street, and plod through that. From basement to sky rise the tenements of an alien colony. Their windows slot the ebony of their walls with lemon. Behind those windows strange life is moving, dressed with forms that are not of London or of England, yet, in essence, the same agreeable life that you have been living, and tonight will live no more. From high above you comes a voice crooning 'The Song of Katta'. Through a window you see a family keeping a religious rite. Through another you see a woman pouring out tea for her husband. You see a man mending a pair of boots; a mother bathing her baby. You have seen all these things before, and never noticed them. You do not notice them now, but if you knew that you were never going to see them again, you would notice them. You never *will* see them again, not because your life has run its natural course, but because a man whom you have often passed in the street has at his own solitary pleasure decided to usurp the awful authority of nature, and destroy you. So perhaps it's as well that you don't notice them, for your part in them is ended. No more for you these pretty moments of our earthly travail: only one moment of terror, and then a plunging darkness.

Closer to you this shadow of massacre moves, and now he is twenty yards behind you. You can hear his footfalls, but you do not turn your head. You are familiar with footfalls.

The Hands of Mr. Ottermole

You are in London, in the easy security of your daily territory, and footfalls behind you, your instinct tells you, are no more than a message of human company.

But can't you hear something in those footfalls—something that goes with a widdershins beat? Something that says: *Look out, look out. Beware, beware.* Can't you hear the very syllables of *murd-er-er-, murd-er-er?* No; there is nothing in footfalls. They are neutral. The foot of villainy falls with the same quiet note as the foot of honesty. But those footfalls, Mr Whybrow, are bearing on to you a pair of hands, and there *is* something in hands. Behind you that pair of hands is even now stretching its muscles in preparation for your end. Every minute of your days you have been seeing human hands. Have you ever realized the sheer horror of hands—those appendages that are a symbol for our moments of trust and affection and salutation? Have you thought of the sickening potentialities that lie within the scope of that five-tentacled member? No, you never have; for all the human hands that you have seen have been stretched to you in kindness or fellowship. Yet, though the eyes can hate, and the lips can sting, it is only that dangling member that can gather the accumulated essence of evil, and electrify it into currents of destruction. Satan may enter into man by many doors, but in the hands alone can he find the servants of his will.

Another minute, Mr Whybrow, and you will know all

about the horror of human hands.

You are nearly home now. You have turned into your street—Caspar Street—and you are in the centre of the chess-board. You can see the front window of your little four-roomed house. The street is dark, and its three lamps give only a smut of light that is more confusing than darkness. It is dark—empty, too. Nobody about; no lights in the front parlours of the houses, for the families are at tea in their kitchens; and only a random glow in a few upper rooms occupied by lodgers. Nobody about but you and your following companion, and you don't notice him. You see him so often that he is never seen. Even if you turned your head and saw him, you would only say 'Good evening' to him, and walk on. A suggestion that he was a possible murderer would not even make you laugh. It would be too silly.

And now you are at your gate. And now you have found your door key. And now you are in, and hanging up your hat and coat. The Missis has just called a greeting from the kitchen, whose smell is an echo of that greeting (herrings!) and you have answered it, when the door shakes under a sharp knock.

Go away, Mr Whybrow. Go away from that door. Don't touch it. Get right away from it. Get out of the house. Run with the Missis to the back garden, and over the fence. Or call the neighbours. But don't touch that door. Don't, Mr

Whybrow, don't open . . .

Mr Whybrow opened the door.

That was the beginning of what became known as London's Strangling Horrors. Horrors they were called because they were something more than murders: they were motiveless, and there was an air of black magic about them. Each murder was committed at a time when the street where the bodies were found was empty of any perceptible or possible murderer. There would be an empty alley. There would be a policeman at its end. He would turn his back on the empty alley for less than a minute. Then he would look round and run into the night with news of another strangling. And in any direction he looked nobody to be seen and no report to be had of anybody being seen. Or he would be on duty in a long quiet street, and suddenly be called to a house of dead people whom a few seconds earlier he had seen alive. And, again, whichever way he looked nobody to be seen; and although police whistles put an immediate cordon around the area, and all houses were searched, no possible murderer to be found.

The first news of the murder of Mr and Mrs Whybrow was brought by the station sergeant. He had been walking through Caspar Street on his way to the station for duty, when he noticed the open door of No 98. Glancing in, he saw by the gaslight of the passage a motionless body on the

12

floor. After a second look he blew his whistle, and when the constables answered him he took one to join him in a search of the house, and sent others to watch all neighbouring streets, and make inquiries at adjoining houses. But neither in the house nor in the streets was anything found to indicate the murderer. Neighbours on either side, and opposite, were questioned, but they had seen nobody about, and had heard nothing. One had heard Mr Whybrow come home—the scrape of his latchkey in the door was so regular an evening sound, he said, that you could set your watch by it for half-past six—but he had heard nothing more than the sound of the opening door until the sergeant's whistle. Nobody had been seen to enter the house or leave it, by front or back, and the necks of the dead people carried no finger-prints or other traces. A nephew was called in to go over the house, but he could find nothing missing; and anyway his uncle possessed nothing worth stealing. The little money in the house was untouched, and there were no signs of any disturbance of the property, or even of struggle. No signs of anything but brutal and wanton murder.

Mr Whybrow was known to neighbours and work-mates as a quiet, likeable, home-loving man; such a man as could not have any enemies. But, then, murdered men seldom have. A relentless enemy who hates a man to the point of wanting to hurt him seldom wants to murder him, since to do that puts him beyond suffering. So the police were left with an impossible situation: no clue to the murderer and no motive for the murders; only the fact that they had been done.

The first news of the affair sent a tremor through London generally, and an electric thrill through all Mallon End. Here was a murder of two inoffensive people, not for gain and not for revenge; and the murderer, to whom, apparently, killing was a casual impulse, was at large. He had left no traces, and, provided he had no companions, there seemed no reason why he should not remain at large. Any clear-headed man who stands alone, and has no fear of God or man, can, if he chooses, hold a city, even a nation, in subjection; but your everyday criminal is seldom clear-headed, and dislikes being lonely. He needs, if not the support of confederates, at least somebody to talk to; his vanity needs the satisfaction of perceiving at first hand the effect of his work. For this he will frequent bars and coffee-shops and other public places. Then, sooner or later, in a glow of comradeship, he will utter the one word too much; and the nark, who is everywhere, has an easy job.

But though the doss-houses and saloons and other places were 'combed' and set with watches, and it was made known by whispers that good money and protection were assured to those with information, nothing attaching to the Whybrow case could be found. The murderer clearly had no friends and kept no company. Known men of this type were called up and questioned, but each was able to give a good account of himself; and in a few days the police were at a dead end. Against the constant public gibe that the thing had been done almost under their noses, they became restive, and for four days each man of the force was working his daily beat under a strain. On the fifth day they became still more restive.

It was the season of annual teas and entertainments for the children of the Sunday Schools, and on an evening of fog, when London was a world of groping phantoms, a small girl, in the bravery of best Sunday frock and shoes, shining face and new-washed hair, set out from Logan Passage for St Michael's Parish Hall. She never got there. She was not actually dead until half-past six, but she was as good as dead from the moment she left her mother's door. Somebody like a man, pacing the street from which the Passage led, saw her come out; and from that moment she was dead. Through the fog somebody's large white hands reached after her, and in fifteen minutes they were about her.

At half-past six a whistle screamed trouble, and those answering it found the body of little Nellie Vrinoff in a warehouse entry in Minnow Street. The sergeant was first among them, and he posted his men to useful points, ordering them here and there in the tart tones of repressed rage, and berating the officer whose beat the street was. 'I saw you, Magson, at the end of the lane. What were you up to there? You were there ten minutes before you turned.' Magson began an explanation about keeping an eye on a suspicious-looking character at that end, but the sergeant cut him short: 'Suspicious characters be damned. You don't want to look for suspicious characters. You want to look for *murderers*. Messing about . . . and then this happens right where you ought to be. Now think what they'll say.'

With the speed of ill news came the crowd, pale and perturbed; and on the story that the unknown monster had appeared again, and this time to a child, their faces streaked the fog with spots of hate and horror. But then came the ambulance and more police, and swiftly they broke up the crowd; and as it broke the sergeant's thought was thickened into words, and from all sides came low murmurs of 'Right under their noses'. Later inquiries showed that four people of the district, above suspicion, had passed that entry at intervals of seconds before the murder, and seen nothing and heard nothing. None of them had passed the child alive or seen her dead. None of them had seen anybody in the street except themselves. Again the police were left with no motive and with no clue.

And now the district, as you will remember, was given

over, not to panic, for the London public never yields to that, but to apprehension and dismay. If these things were happening in their familiar streets, then anything might happen. Wherever people met—in the streets, the markets and the shops—they debated the one topic. Women took to bolting their windows and doors at the first fall of dusk. They kept their children closely under their eye. They did their shopping before dark, and watched anxiously, while pretending they weren't watching, for the return of their husbands from work. Under the Cockney's semi-humorous resignation to disaster, they hid an hourly foreboding. By the whim of one man with a pair of hands the structure and tenor of their daily life were shaken, as they always can be shaken by any man contemptuous of humanity and fearless of its laws. They began to realize that the pillars that supported the peaceable society in which they lived were mere straws that anybody could snap; that laws were powerful only so long as they were obeyed; that the police were potent only so long as they were feared. By the power of his hands this one man had made a whole community do something new: he had made it think, and left it gasping at the obvious.

And then, while it was yet gasping under his first two strokes, he made his third. Conscious of the horror that his hands had created, and hungry as an actor who has once tasted the thrill of the multitude, he made fresh advertisement of his presence; and on Wednesday morning, three days after the murder of the child, the papers carried to the breakfast-tables of England the story of a still more shocking outrage.

At 9.32 on Tuesday night a constable was on duty in Jarnigan Road, and at that time spoke to a fellow-officer named Petersen at the top of Clemming Street. He had seen this officer walk down that street. He could swear that the street was empty at that time, except for a lame boot-black whom he knew by sight, and who passed him and entered a tenement on the side opposite that on which his fellow-officer was walking. He had the habit, as all constables had just then, of looking constantly behind him and around him, whichever way he was walking, and he was certain that the street was empty. He passed his sergeant at 9.33, saluted him, and answered his inquiry for anything seen. He reported that he had seen nothing, and passed on. His beat ended at a short distance from Clemming Street, and, having paced it, he turned and came again at 9.34 to the top of the street. He had scarcely reached it before he heard the hoarse voice of the sergeant: 'Gregory! You there? Quick. Here's another. My God, it's Petersen! Garotted. Quick, call 'em up!'

That was the third of the Strangling Horrors, of which there were to be a fourth and a fifth; and the five horrors were to pass into the unknown and unknowable. That is,

18

unknown as far as authority and the public were concerned. The identity of the murderer *was* known, but to two men only. One was the murderer himself; the other was a young journalist.

This young man, who was covering the affairs for his paper, the *Daily Torch*, was no smarter than the other zealous newspaper men who were hanging about these byways in the hope of a sudden story. But he was patient, and he hung a little closer to the case than the other fellows and by continually staring at it he at last raised the figure of the murderer like a genie from the stones on which he had stood to do his murders.

After the first few days the men had given up any attempt at exclusive stories, for there was none to be had. They met regularly at the police station, and what little information there was they shared. The officials were agreeable to them, but no more. The sergeant discussed with them the details of each murder; suggested possible explanations of the man's methods; recalled from the past those cases that had some similarity; and on the matter of motive reminded them of the motiveless Neil Cream and the wanton John Williams, and hinted that work was being done which would soon bring the business to an end; but about that work he would not say a word. The Inspector, too, was gracefully garrulous on the theme of Murder, but whenever one of the party edged the talk towards what was being done in this immediate matter, he glided past it. Whatever the officials knew, they were not giving it to newspaper men. The business had fallen heavily upon them, and only by a capture made by their own efforts could they rehabilitate themselves in official and public esteem. Scotland Yard, of course, was at work, and had all the station's material; but the station's hope was that they themselves would have the honour of settling the affair; and however useful the co-operation of the Press might be in other cases, they did not want to risk a defeat by a premature disclosure of their theories and plans.

So the sergeant talked at large, and propounded one interesting theory after another, all of which the newspaper men had thought of themselves.

The young man soon gave up these morning lectures on the Philosophy of Crime, and took to wandering about the streets and making bright stories out of the effect of the murders on the normal life of the people. A melancholy job made more melancholy by the district. The littered roadways, the crestfallen houses, the bleared windows—all held the acid misery that evokes no sympathy: the misery of the frustrated poet. The misery was the creation of the aliens, who were living in this makeshift fashion because they had no settled homes, and would neither take the trouble to make a home where they *could* settle, nor get on with their wandering.

There was little to be picked up. All he saw and heard were indignant faces, and wild conjectures of the murderer's identity and of the secret of his trick of appearing and disappearing unseen. Since a policeman himself had fallen a victim, denunciations of the force had ceased, and the unknown was now invested with a cloak of legend. Men eyed other men, as though thinking: It might be *him*. It might be *him*. They were no longer looking for a man who had the air of a Madame Tussaud murderer; they were looking for a man, or perhaps some harridan woman, who had done these particular murders. Their thoughts ran mainly on the foreign set. Such ruffianism could scarcely belong to England, nor could the bewildering cleverness of the thing. So they turned to Rumanian gipsies and Turkish carpet-sellers. There, clearly, would be found the 'warm' spot. These Eastern fellows—they knew all sorts of tricks, and they had no real religion—nothing to hold them within bounds. Sailors returning from those parts had told tales of conjurers who made themselves invisible; and there were tales of Egyptian and Arab potions that were used for abysmally queer purposes. Perhaps it *was* possible to them; you never knew. They were so slick and cunning, and they had such gliding movements; no Englishman could melt away as they could. Almost certainly the murderer would be found to be one of that sort—with some dark trick of his own—and

21

just because they were sure that he *was* a magician, they felt that it was useless to look for him. He was a power, able to hold them in subjection and to hold himself untouchable. Superstition, which so easily cracks the frail shell of reason, had got into them. He could do anything he chose; he would never be discovered. These two points they settled, and they went about the streets in a mood of resentful fatalism.

They talked of their ideas to the journalist in half-tones, looking right and left, as though *HE* might overhear them and visit them. And though all the district was thinking of him and ready to pounce upon him, yet, so strongly had he worked upon them, that if any man in the street—say, a small man of commonplace features and form—had cried '*I am the Monster!*' would their stifled fury have broken into flood and have borne him down and engulfed him? Or would they not suddenly have seen something unearthly in that everyday face and figure, something unearthly in his everyday boots, something unearthly about his hat, something that marked him as one whom none of their weapons could alarm or pierce? And would they not momentarily have fallen back from this devil, as the devil fell back from the Cross made by the sword of Faust, and so have given him time to escape? I do not know; but so fixed was their belief in his invincibility that it is at least likely that they would have made this hesitation, had such an occasion arisen. But it never did.

Today this commonplace fellow, his murder lust glutted, is still seen and observed among them as he was seen and observed all the time; but because nobody then dreamt, or now dreams, that he was what he was, they observed him then, and observe him now, as people observe a lamp-post.

Almost was their belief in his invincibility justified; for five days after the murder of the policeman Petersen, when the experience and inspiration of the whole detective force of London were turned towards his identification and capture, he made his fourth and fifth strokes.

At nine o'clock that evening, the young newspaper man, who hung about every night until his paper was away, was strolling along Richards Lane. Richards Lane is a narrow street, partly a stall-market, and partly residential. The young man was in the residential section, which carries on one side small working-class cottages, and on the other the wall of a railway goods yard. The great wall hung a blanket of shadow over the lane, and the shadow and the cadaverous outline of the now deserted market stalls gave it the appearance of a living lane that had been turned to frost in the moment between breath and death. The very lamps, that elsewhere were nimbuses of gold, had here the rigidity of gems. The journalist, feeling this message of frozen eternity, was telling himself that he was tired of the whole thing, when in one stroke the frost was broken. In the moment between one pace and another silence and darkness were racked by a high scream and through the screams a voice: 'Help! help! *He's here!*

Before he could think what movement to make, the lane came to life. As though its invisible populace had been waiting on that cry, the door of every cottage was flung open, and from them and from the alleys poured shadowy figures bent in question-mark form. For a second or so they stood as rigid as the lamps; then a police whistle gave them direction, and the flock of shadows sloped up the street. The journalist followed them, and others followed him. From the main street and from surrounding streets they came, some risen from unfinished suppers, some disturbed in their ease of slippers and shirtsleeves, some stumbling on infirm limbs, and some upright, and armed with pokers or the tools of their trade. Here and there above the wavering cloud of heads moved the bold helmets of policemen. In one dim mass they surged upon a cottage whose doorway was marked by the sergeant and two constables; and voices of those behind urged them on with 'Get in! Find him! Run round the back! Over the wall!' and those in front cried: 'Keep back! Keep back!'

And now the fury of a mob held in thrall by unknown peril broke loose. He was here—on the spot. Surely this time he *could not* escape. All minds were bent upon the cottage;

all energies thrust towards its doors and windows and roof; all thought was turned upon one unknown man and his extermination. So that no one man saw any other man. No man saw the narrow, packed lane and the mass of struggling shadows, and all forgot to look among themselves for the monster who never lingered upon his victims. All forgot, indeed, that they, by their mass crusade of vengeance, were affording him the perfect hiding place. They saw only the house, and they heard only the rending of woodwork and the smash of glass at back and front, and the police giving orders or crying with the chase; and they pressed on.

But they found no murderer. All they found was news of murder and a glimpse of the ambulance, and for their fury there was no other object than the police themselves, who fought against this hampering of their work.

The journalist managed to struggle though to the cottage door, and to get the story from the constable stationed there. The cottage was the home of a pensioned sailor and his wife and daughter. They had been at supper, and at first it appeared that some noxious gas had smitten all three in mid-action. The daughter lay dead on the hearthrug, with a piece of bread and butter in her band. The father had fallen sideways from his chair, leaving on his plate a filled spoon of rice-pudding. The mother lay half under the table, her lap filled with the pieces of a broken cup and splashes of cocoa. But in three seconds the idea of gas was dismissed. One glance at their necks showed that this was the Strangler again; and the police stood and looked at the room and momentarily shared the fatalism of the public. They were helpless.

This was his fourth visit, making seven murders in all. He was to do, as you know, one more—and to do it that night; and then he was to pass into history as the unknown London horror, and return to the decent life that he had always led, remembering little of what he had done, and worried not at all by the memory. Why did he stop? Impossible to say. Why did he begin? Impossible again. It just happened like that; and if he thinks at all of those days and nights, I surmise that he thinks of them as we think of foolish or dirty little sins that we committed in childhood. We say that they were not really sins, because we were not then consciously ourselves: we had not come to realization; and we look back at that foolish little creature that we once were, and forgive him because he didn't know. So, I think, with this man.

There are plenty like him. Eugèene Aram, after the murder of Daniel Clark, lived a quiet, contented life for fourteen years, unhaunted by his crime and unshaken in his self-esteem. Dr Crippen murdered his wife, and then lived pleasantly with his mistress in the house under whose floor he had buried his wife. Constance Kent, found Not Guilty of the murder of her young brother, led a peaceful life for five years before she confessed. George Joseph Smith and William Palmer lived amiably among their fellows untroubled by fear or by remorse for their poisonings and drownings. Charles Peace, at the time he made his one unfortunate essay, had settled down into a respectable citizen with an interest in antiques. It happened that, after a lapse of time, these men were discovered, but more murderers than we guess are living decent lives today, and will die in decency, undiscovered and unsuspected. As this man will.

But he had a narrow escape, and it was perhaps this narrow escape that brought him to a stop. The escape was due to an error of judgment on the part of the journalist.

As soon as he had the full story of the affair, which took some time, he spent fifteen minutes on the telephone, sending the story through, and at the end of the fifteen minutes, when the stimulus of the business had left him, he felt physically tired and mentally dishevelled. He was not yet free to go home; the paper would not go away for another hour; so he turned into a bar for a drink and some sandwiches.

It was then, when he had dismissed the whole business from his mind, and was looking about the bar and admiring the landlord's taste in watch-chains and his air of domination, and was thinking that the landlord of a well-conducted tavern had a more comfortable life than a newspaper man, that his mind received from nowhere a spark of light. He was not thinking about the Strangling Horrors; his mind was on his sandwich. As a public-house sandwich, it was a curiosity. The bread had been thinly cut, it was buttered, and the ham was not two months stale; it was ham as it should be. His mind turned to the inventor of this refreshment, the Earl of Sandwich, and then to George the Fourth, and then to the Georges, and to the legend of that George who was worried to know how the apple got into the apple-dumpling. He worried whether George would have been equally puzzled to know how the ham got into the ham sandwich, and how long it would have been before it occurred to him that the ham could not have got there unless somebody had put it there. He got up to order another sandwich, and in that moment a little active corner of his mind settled the affair. If there was ham in his sandwich, somebody must have put it there. If seven people had been murdered, somebody must have been there to murder them. There was no aeroplane or automobile that would go into a man's pocket; therefore that somebody must have escaped either by running away or standing still; and again therefore—

He was visualizing the front page story that his paper would carry if his theory were correct, and if—a matter of conjecture—his editor had the necessary nerve to make a bold stroke, when a cry of 'Time, gentleman, please! All out!' reminded him of the hour. He got up and went out into a world of mist, broken by the ragged discs of roadside puddles and the streaming lightning of motor buses. He was certain that he had *the* story, but, even if it were proved, he was doubtful whether the policy of his paper would permit him to print it. It had one great fault. It was truth, but it was impossible truth. It rocked the foundations of everything that newspaper readers believed and that newspaper editors helped them to believe. They might believe that Turkish carpet-sellers had the gift of making themselves invisible. They would not belive this.

As it happened, they were not asked to, for the story was never written. As his paper had by now gone away, and as he was nourished by his refreshment and stimulated by his theory, he thought he might put in an extra half-hour by testing that theory. So he began to look about for the man he had in mind—a man with white hair, and large white hands; otherwise an everyday figure whom nobody would look twice at. He wanted to spring his idea on this man without warning, and he was going to place himself within reach of a man armoured in legends of dreadfulness and grue. This might appear to be an act of supreme courage—that one man, with no hope of immediate outside support, should place himself at the mercy of one who was holding a whole parish in terror. But it wasn't. He didn't think about the risk. He didn't think about his duty to his employers or loyalty to his paper. He was moved simply by an instinct to follow a story to its end.

He walked slowly from the tavern and crossed into Fingal Street, making for Deever Market, where he had hope of finding his man. But his journey was shortened. At the corner of Lotus Street he saw him—or a man who looked like him. This street was poorly lit, and he could see little of the man: but he *could* see white hands. For some twenty paces he stalked him; then drew level with him; and at a point where the arch of a railway crossed the street, he saw that this was his man. He approached him with the current conversational phrase of the district: 'Well, seen anything of the murderer?' The man stopped to look sharply at him, then, satisfied that the journalist was not the murderer, said:

'Eh? No, nor's anybody else, curse it. Doubt if they ever will.'

'I don't know. I've been thinking about them, and I've got an idea.'

'So?'

'Yes. Came to me all of a sudden. Quarter of an hour ago. And I'd felt that we'd all been blind. It's been staring us in the face.'

The man turned again to look at him, and the look and

the movement held suspicion of this man who seemed to know so much. 'Oh? Has it? Well, if you're so sure, why not give us the benefit of it?'

'I'm going to.' They walked level, and were nearly at the end of the little street where it meets Deever Market, when the journalist turned casually to the man. He put a finger on his arm. 'Yes, it seems to me quite simple now. But there's still one point I don't understand. One little thing I'd like to clear up. I mean the motive. Now, as man to man, tell me, Sergeant Ottermole, just *why* did you kill those inoffensive people?'

The sergeant stopped, and the journalist stopped. There was just enough light from the sky, which held the reflected light of the continent of London, to give him a sight of the sergeant's face, and the sergeant's face was turned to him with a wide smile of such urbanity and charm that the journalist's eyes were frozen as they met it. The smile stayed for some seconds. Then said the sergeant: 'Well, to tell you the truth, Mister Newspaper Man, I don't know. I really don't know. In fact, I've been worried about it myself. But I've got an idea—just like you. Everybody knows that we can't control the workings of our minds. Don't they? Ideas come into our minds without asking. But everybody's supposed to be able to control his body. Why? Eh? We get our minds from lord-knows-where—from people who were dead hundreds of years before we were born. Mayn't we get our bodies in the same way? Our faces—our legs—our heads—they aren't completely ours. We don't make 'em. They come to us. And couldn't ideas come into our bodies like ideas come into our minds? Eh? Can't ideas live in nerve and muscle as well as in brain? Couldn't it be that parts of our bodies aren't really us, and couldn't ideas come into those parts all of a sudden, like ideas come into—into'—he shot his arms out, showing the great white-gloved hands and hairy wrists; shot them out so swiftly to the journalist's throat that his eyes never saw them—'into *my hands!*'

Lightning Source UK Ltd.
Milton Keynes UK
UKOW02f1706211116

288166UK00001B/340/P